Journey To Heaven

Presented by-Bshayar52

Compiler:

Kumkum Priyadarshini Sahu

DISCLAIMER

This is a work of fiction. Our editors have tried their best to edit the content of all the author/authors and check the plagiarism. All the write-ups in this book are unique and are only published in this book.

In case any plagiarism or error is found, the author is the sole responsible and not the publisher.

ACKNOWLEDGEMENTS

First and foremost, I would like to thank God.

In the process of putting this book together I realized how true this gift of writing is for me. You have given me the power to believe in my passion and pursue my dreams. I could never have done this without the faith I have in ALMIGHTY.

Now, I thank my parents. I can barely find the words to express all the wisdom, love and support they have given to me.

I would like to thank all of my family members for trusting me and thank to my entire writer's family who helped me in every phase of my life.

I thank BOOK SQUIRREL PUBLICATIONS team for providing this beautiful platform for writers.

I THANK ALL MY CO WRITERS WHO WORK TOGETHER AND MAKE THIS BEAUTIFUL PIECE.

Right now whatever I am is because of all the sacrifices of my parents, family and friends.

Prakriti Bhagat

Prakriti bhagat is an infamous writer who belongs to Jaipur. Currently she is working in Rajasthan High court and her hobbies include writing and photography along with crafting. Her writing intrest belongs to the life she has gone through or have felt of others.

तुम्हारे साथ चलना कुछ ऐसा है
जैसे चांद और चांदनी का साथ चलना
नदी और समुद्र का मिलना।

ये क्या बात हुइ तुम यूं खफा हो गए
हम यहां इंतजार करते रहे
तुम कहीं और गुफ्तगू करते रहे।

जहां दिल लगाया जाता है
वहां दिमाग नहीं लगाया जाता
दिमाग अक्सर रिश्तों में फायदा देखता है।
-Prakriti Bhagat

तुम्हे क्या हुआ
होने तो उसे था
जिसका तुमने दिल तोड़ा
जिसके तुमने सपने तोड़े
जिसको तुमने ठुकराया।

सबकी अपनी दुनिया है
जिसमें हम होकर भी नहीं होते
इसलिए अपनी दुनिया में ही
खुश रहना अच्छा है।

यादों की भी अजीब तकदीर है
अच्छी बुरी दोनों इंसान पर निर्भर करती है।
- Prakriti Bhagat

साहिल पर खड़े होकर
तूफान से बैर नी रखते
पता नहीं कब कोनसा तूफान
ज़िन्दगी का रुख बदल दे।

जितना है उतना काफी है
ज्यादा कि आरज़ू में

कहीं वह भी हाथ से
रेत की तरह फिसल ना जाए।

पहले तो उसूलों पर चला करती थी दुनिया
अब तो वादे भी बेमैयने हैं।
- Prakriti Bhagat
दुआ की बारिश काश मुझ पर भी होती
खुदा से बस एक ही दुआ मांगती
तेरा सजदा ताउम्र करती रहूं।

आज फिर आती है तेरी याद

जैसे आयि हो नदी को सागर की याद
जमीन को बारिश की याद।

नई सुबह नई शरुआत
बस कुछ पुराना है तो
मै और तुम्हारी याद।
- Prakriti Bhagat

वक़्त के हाथों इतने मजबूर हुए
भूल हि गए कौन अपने थे
कौन पराए थे।

तेरे इश्क़ का गुरूर
कुछ यूं सर चढकर बोला
दुनिया से मुंह मोड़ लिया।

दिल टूटने की आवाज़ जितनी
ज़माने के सामने खामोश होती है
उतनी ही खुद के कानों में गूंजती है।

Gargi Goel

Her name is Gargi Goel. She was born on 29th July 1980 and her birth place is Hissar, Haryana. Her father and other hindi poets as Harivansh Rai Bachchan, Subhadra Kumaari Chauhaan, Ramdhari Singh Dinkar...inspired her to write poems. She has done MBBS and MD pediatrics.

Now a days she is working as Primary health Physician in rural areas.

Her pen name is "Kusumanratan".

<u>परियों का देश</u>
परियों के देश में
जी को अपने बहलाना, पर
लौट आना
साँझ होते लौट आना
दूर देश में सुनना,
परियों का मधुर गाना
रंग बिरंगे फूलों को देखना
खिल खिल कर मुस्कुराना
बेलों के झूले पर झूलना

बादलों के संग नील गगन में उड़ जाना
सूरज की प्रखर किरणों पर
सतरंगी इन्द्रधनुष बन जाना
सुनना चिड़ियों का भोर में चहचाना
कल – कल करती नदियों का छलछलाना
हे ईश्वर! एसे ही तुम
हम सबके जीवन को महकाना
-Gargi Goel

<u>पार्टी</u>

एक जमघट लगा कोने में
पुते चेहरों के साथ झिलमिल करते लिबास
अंगों में फँसे गहनें सोने के
हँसी चेहरों पर चिपकाई हुई
और बिक रहा सम्मान सामान सा यहाँ
चिलचिलाती रोशनी
जो कालिमा चमकदार कर दे
ख़ामोशी जो
मन में शोर मचा दे

सद्भाव का मीठा ज़हर
वातावरण में घुला हुआ
दिखावा (आडम्बर) सभी को जैसे
विरासत में मिला हुआ
विविध व्यंजन जहां सजे हुए
ढेरों पकवान जहां बिखरे हुए
जिव्हा को ललचाने वाले
कष्ट देह को देने वाले
हँसी ठट्टा, चर्चा और चिल्लाहट
माहौल में गूँज रहे

मातम सी चुप्पी छाई
लगता मन को यही
आनंदित हो भोजन करना और
दोहरे आनंद से 'झूठ' छोड़ना
सजी सजाई थाली को झूठ में बनाकर
स्वयं को मित्तभोजी समझ गर्वित होना
सडी गली बातों की बास में नहाती पार्टी
पार्टी के शौक़ीन ज़रा समझ ले
समय जो ये बर्बाद करे इतना
भोजन का महत्व नहीं जहां पर

पूछे उन भूखों से जाकर
जिनके पेट की ज्वाला दिनों दिन शांत नहीं हुई
ये स्वाद के मारे, देखे वे बेचारे
जिन्हें स्वाद का ज्ञान तक नहीं
झूठन भी जो भोग समझ खा जाए
और झूठन छोड़ पार्टी वाले अपनी शान बढ़ाएं

-Gargi Goel

शायरियां

ज़िंदगी ख्वाब है कौन इसे रचता नहीं
और जो सच हो जाए तो कोई इसे समझता नहीं

-Gargi Goel

कौन है वो जो मौत से डरता नहीं
और जो न डरे सच है के कभी मरता नहीं

-Gargi Goel

कौन है वो जो खुशियों में बहकता नहीं
और सच है इंसान, गिर कर संभालता नहीं

-Gargi Goel

कौन है जो इस जहां के गुलशन में चहकता नहीं
और मानिए कि हर कोई फूल बन महकता नहीं
-Gargi Goel

कई है जिनका मन ज़िंदगी से भरता नहीं
और मौत मांगे जो जुबां से, मन से उसके ख्वाब जीने का मरता
नहीं
-Gargi Goel

रोते बिलखते किसी से कारवां चलता नहीं
और जो हँस के चल दिए तो सिलसिला कभी ये रुकता नहीं
-Gargi Goel

कौन है जिसे अपनी शौहरत से उल्फ़त नहीं
और जो पा जाए इसे तो क्या ख़ुदा से फुरकत नहीं
ख़ुदा से नाख़ुश क्यूँ है वो जिनकी क़िस्मत अच्छी नहीं
और जो खुश है, क्या उनमें क़िस्मत बदलने की हिम्मत नहीं
-Gargi Goel

हमको तो अपने ग़मों से मिली फुर्सत नहीं
और जो शामिल है औरों के ग़मों में, क्या खुशियों में हुई
हरक़त नहीं
-Gargi Goel

यूँ तो कुछ कर गुज़रने की किसमें हसरत नहीं
पर वहीं हमारे दिल में बची खुदा के लिए चाहत नही
-Gargi Goel

जिव्हा

मानव अब जीव नहीं रहा

मानव मात्र जिव्हा बन गया

वाणी हो उसकी पहचान

मात्र रह गई है

भावनाएं उसकी खामोशी सी

दब कर रह गई है मानव का कर्म भी बंध गया है
शब्दों की जटाओं से
क्रियाएं सारी हो चुकी शिथिल
वर्णों को ज़र्द हवाओं से
चेतना मानव की जिव्हा तक
सीमित हो गई है
जिव्हा ही अब मानव हो गई
मस्तिष्क भी हो चुका जिव्हा का गुलाम
किन्तु मूक रहना भी तो है एक जवाब

मानव पंच तत्वों का एक सम्पूर्ण रूप है
जिव्हा मानव का अंग है ना की मानव जिव्हा का
 -Gargi Goel

कछुआ चाल

धीरे धीरे चलती है हमारी ज़िंदगी
तो लोग एतराज़ जताते है
बड़े ताव में आकर समझाते है
"यूँ नहीं चलेगा, यूँ करलो
तेज़ रफ़्तार से बंदगी"

बचपन में कछुए और खरगोश की
कहानी कुछ यूँ भा गई
कि कछुए पर फ़िदा हो गए और फिर
धीरे धीरे और धीरे ही हो गए
चूहा दौड़ में अक्सर खरगोश ही है
तेज़ फुदकते है और दूर जाकर
जब नज़र नजर ना आते है, सुस्ताते है
आराम फरमाते है
उनका सुस्ताता ना ही दर्शाता है
मंज़िल उनकी कछुए को हराना है

जीत की रेखा के पार ना उनको जाना है
कछुए कप तो रेखा पार जाना है
न किसी खरगोश को हराना है
हमने अपनी कमजोरियों के साथ चलना सीख लिया है
इसलिए कछुआ जात में खुद को दाखिल कर लिया है
थकना हमारा काम नहीं, हम सुस्ताते नहीं
क्यूंकि हमारी चाल तो सुस्त है
किन्तु इरादे चुस्त है

खरगोश की भाँती हम चाल पर इतराते नहीं
धीरे धीरे तो धीरे की ही उपज है
नर्म, मुलायम, रोएंदार धवल खरगोश बड़े
तीव्र होते है
किन्तु सख्त खोल में अटके मटमैले
कछुए क्या कम जीवंत होते है
धीरे ही सही पर बड़े धैर्यवान भी होते है
फ़िर अधीर हो क्यूं खरगोश जैसे अभिमानी
हो जाए
मंज़िल पाने से पहले नींद की गोद में

चले जाए
कभी न रुकना, कभी न थकना चलते रहना
धीरपुरुष हूँ, कच्छप जात, बिन उन्माद
मंजिल पार लूँगा विराम
मंद गति हूँ मंद बुद्धि नहीं, सुस्त चाल हूँ सुस्त हाल नहीं
धीमे धीमे हौले हौले बस बढ़ते जा जाए
प्रसन्न चित्त हो हम विलंबित राग में गाए
देर सवेर तो सब सापेक्षता के तले दबा है

खुद को पाना, जाना जाना चलते जाना बस यही मंसूबा है
जीवन पथ को क्यारों में निहार निहार
हर क़दम बढाए फिर क्यूं तेज़ गति में आकर हम क्षत विक्षत
हो जाए
अरे क्यूँ खड़ा होता है ये सारा बवाल
किस बात आखिर कछुए को मलाल
जिस जीत के पीछे ये दुनिया भागती है
अंत में वो जीत कछुए के हिस्से में आती है
-Gargi Goel

Nabajit Chatterjee

Nabajit is a published freelance writer and poet. Born and brought in the land of the rising sun, Arunachal Pradesh, Nabajit finds his inner peace while pouring his feelings into poetic words.His work surrounds situations and emotions of human behavior beautifully amalgamated with nature.He has a keen interest in history and culture . Apart from writing, he enjoys reading,playing keyboard and listening to music. He has been staying in Bangalore for the past three years. He is a member of Bangalore Poetry Circle.

A Rainy Walk

Dribbling down are the silver droplets
From our clasped umbrellas
As we walk together in the pouring rain.
Leaves clattered as if etched,
Along the velvety black pitched lane.
Between us the cold whispering wind gushes,
Sprinkles of droplet upon us it splashes.
The transient rapturous smile of her
Elevates the ardor of untarnished love.
Relinquished of all desires,

Tranced in the hypnosis of beauty,
I see silhouette of rain drops,
Upon her gleaming eyes,
Drenching me in sublime drizzles of serenity.
-Nabajit Chatterjee

The Stream of Time

The stream of time ,
Cascades down the memory lane,
Drenches the pilgrim soul.
It revives the faded fragment of memories,
Like the withered leaves ,

Which lay dormant in their solitude,
Preserved in an unknown dwelling place
And were long forgotten in the race.
Kneeling, I look at my reflection,
Each leaf shows a different me,
Each leaf casts a vivid images
Of someone I used to be.
One of toddler giggling
As the bubbles of rain
Drip upon the tip of nose,
Others of timid adolescent boy,

Consumed by the dilemma
Whether or not to offer her the red rose.
Overwhelmed with nostalgia ,
Contemplating over the thoughts of glee,
Long had I forgotten ,
I am made up of many me,
I am made up of many me !
-Nabajit Chatterjee

Tipsy Clouds

The enchanting view of clouds
Drowns me in its exquisiteness.

The sea of white rises above

Taking various shapes ,indifferent to the surroundings.

Flying high like a tipsy soul

Being carried away by the wind,

Carefree, letting itself to be taken,

Powerful yet docile.

Overburdened, puffing ,trying to calm down,

as if it were a panting heart,

Unsure of which emotions to keep

And which ones to let go.

-Nabajit Chatterjee

Silver Lining of dark Clouds

Trembles the moon as the storm welcomes,
Dressed in silver , the knights of dark clouds,
Galloping in haste to conquer the night sky,
To drench the ground,
To drench the chasms of humanity.
Testimonies are the empty roads,
The nature reclaims it solitude,
And looking down,
Smiles the waning moon

As it sees among the window panes,
Some of gold others of wood,
Ambivalent eyes ,gazing each other stood.
-Nabajit Chatterjee

Path to the Stars

The desire of her glimpse,
Sails over me.
Among the lamps of the lonely roads,
I meander in my perpetual seclusion.
My desire oils these lamps,
Carrying me to an imbecile pursuit,

Where the lamps glowing
Mingle with the stars.
Now I peek as much as I desire,
And for her ! nothing changes,
except in her sky full of stars,
One particular , twinkles brighter than the fire,
Healing all her scars.

-Nabajit Chatterjee

Asande Ntobela

His name is Asande Ntobela from South Africa, currently a student at the University of KwaZulu Natal. His failures and lonliness brought him to the world of writing, it's a place where he could attain emotional balance and self-motivation. He is inspired by short but heavy poetry.

Family Apart.

A deviation of was supposed
to be a unified bond.
An angry mother the testicle,
The womb is disheartened.
A forbidden sight. The blood has lost.
-Asande Ntobela

A one word memory: Father

Strangers gathering and crying I can't say the feeling is
mutual.
It's not Hate, but the relationship we had - it

was numb, no emotions, you killed it.

The dusty streets can tell you,

I waited every Christmas, till time gave up. No sight of you.

Every New Year's Eve, hope you person, hope. My firework shooting a hundred wishes, may you return I just had a wet dream.

They say I should wtite your obituary -

I did take drama classes in school (so you know) but this script I can't memorize.

Farewell, thanks for the gift but not what was in it. My eyes are dry, no precipitation, what's the point anyway, you never heared my cries when you still could. Maybe I'm heartless.

-Asande Ntobela

An end to start.

My Father's cane hand, had died.
As it can't hold, I hold it.
It looked really tough alive,
Now it's tender.
-Asande Ntobela

Forgive: Fracture be life of us.

Beaten to fold,
one gives pattern to other,
and the chain is strong.

Although eventually one would
rub the other to thin, the purpose
and function be achieved.

-Asande Ntobela

Grown Apart

At least when we are done,
our leaves will drop and kiss.
As dirt we'll be fertile to land,
Others like us shall grow in our
Efforts, hang in there my love...

-Asande Ntobela

Ibrahim Ali Rasso

His name is Ibrahim Ali Rasso. He was born in feb. 16,1998. He is 22 years old, a Christian. He comes from city Mombasa of Kenya. Africa is his mother continent. Nowadays he is living alone and currently studying ICT. He loves writing and drawing. He is also a pencil artist.

He has four Muslim brothers and one Christian sister. He grew in other town than Mombasa and nowadays he is in search of a new home. His mother died in 2005 and for that he lived with his siblings finding their way.

Dear God

I lost count on the number,

The number of days since Corona took over,

It's another day I humble myself,

Due to economy I get not much on food shelf,

I have few things to call mine,

But I can't complain, my health is fine,

The Corona symptoms are like a myth in my body,

I am grateful, and if I complained God am sorry,

I don't wanna ask for anything,
I just wanna thank you for everything,
Keep on keeping my family safe,
Also my friends close and far,
To you God am thankful and grateful,
I don't know where all this is heading to but I trust you
-Ibrahim Ali Rasso

Fell but rose...

My kingdom crumbled,
The people I called mine, my love gambled,
They didn't care how fragile my heart was,

Just like tributaries they all took their courses
I ain't blaming no soul for I was to blame,
Instead of keeping it real I did let them play me, a game,
But what happens now?
I'mma pull my shit together and start a new kingdom,
I'mma hustle up and get myself a crown,
But I don't wanna be a king, I wanna be the fierce wolf,
The lone one, no more pack hunting.
It's sad that knock down is not a knock out,

I'mma get back in the ring,
I wanna work in silence, I won't bark or shout,
Slowly I'll build what I lost,
I'll earn no matter the cost!
-Ibrahim Ali Rasso

A cry to God... Covid

I rest my case,
Am even reducing the pace,
Talk about that are dope and ace,
I can't make it to where am going I guess.

I wanna see my city crowded again,
I miss the markets with the urge to bargain,
I wanna knock myself to Church and dump my burdens,
I wanna meet my friends, him and her like wherever,
I can' take it anymore because it's taking forever.
Dear God please intervene,
Forgive us and take away Corona scene,
It has changed a lot, something never seen,
Work at home, there are no jobs there,
Stay at home, hunger and boredom takes me

back to the store,
Sanitize the hands, that's great but the soap, water and
money are running out,
Clearly the tunnel we are in feels long,
The light at the and of it seems long gone,
No matter what happens our will stand,
East or West our trust will fall to you God,
We are losing the once we love,
We are weakening day in and day out
Dear God, stand with us,
Dear Lord, strengthen us,

Let the blood at Calvary flow,
Let it nourish us and make us glow
-Ibrahim Ali Rasso

47

Street to seat love

I bless the day we met,
Walking at the park with your pet,
Of course at first I appeared as a threat,
I was running towards being chased for a debt,
Stumbled and fell on your feet,
You quickly gave undivided attention,
You paid my debt and settled the case...

From the streets,
You brought me to a ghetto with seats,
Still confused if it's a dream or reality,
 You changed my I life in a blink,
Got me cleaned and dressed up,
The mob said am just another street thief,
But you cared less and helped no beef,
I had no work experience but I had talent,
I sang for you Everytime you came home,
Slowly you fell for me,
Pulled me from rags to riches,

Walked with me to all the beaches…
Am sorry now have to go,
You didn't realize what the street did to me,
You covered me with love,
I even didn't realize I was sick,
Am on a hospital bed,
Doc said I don't have much time,
I can't bare to see tears in your eyes,
Oh, yeah, I remember you ain't too good at good-byes,
But smile my love,
Cause love will find you again.
-Ibrahim Ali Rasso

I deserved it...

She gave me a key, and I lost it,
She gave me a heart, and I broke it,
I gave her promise, and failed her,
I asked for second chances, and I screwed up,
I apologized, and she forgave me,
I lied, she understood, she smiled...
But at the end she left me,
She was strong, but not ready to be used,
She was brave to fight for me, but not herself,

She was patient to wait, but not to mess,
She tired to entertain, and slowly she gave up,
But do I blame her?
Should I hate her?
Is she wrong?
No, I deserve it.
-Ibrahim Ali Rasso

Mahi Pamnani

I am mahi and was born on 2nd March 2002 in Madhubani, Bihar.I presently a student in standard 12. I love to read, write and do yoga.I do not exactly know why I started writing but I remember one day I had a lot inside of me and I needed to get them out, so I wrote and since that day I have been writing. I also believe everyone has a story and who they are and how they are has a reason.

I'm tired...
I'm tired of this race,
The race in this world.
I'm tired...
I'm tired of proving,
Proving that I can be something.
I'm tired...
I'm tired of this world,
World with no humanity.
I'm tired...
I'm tired of telling,

Telling people to live.
I'm tired...
I'm tired of living,
Living in this emotionless world.
I'm tired...
I'm tired of the people,
People who are no more humans.
-Mahi

Here I am for you.
All you have to do...
Is give a knock.

Here I am for you.
All you have to do...
Is ask for help.
Here I am for you.
All you have to do...
Is speak to me.
Here I am for you.
All you have to do...
Is hold my hand.
Here I am for you.
All you have to do...

Is tell me about it.
Here I am for you.
All you have to do...
Is knock at my door.

-Mahi

She was a little girl with beautiful dreams,
But your glare...
Made them nightmares.
She was like a blossomed flower,
But your touch...
Shredded her.
She was warmth of the winter sun,

But your darkness...
Made them long cold nights.
She was full of innocence,
But your vision...
Took them away from her.
She was like a warm breeze of autumn,
But your cold breeze...
Froze her.
She was a beautiful lady with a pure heart,
But your actions...
Shattered her, scared her and disgusted her.
-Mahi

I need you to be,
The sunshine to my darkness
Cause I can't take it anymore.
I need you to,
Fix my broken heart
Cause I can't hold it anymore.
I need you to be,
The path of my puzzle
Cause I can't be lost anymore.
I need you to,
Hug me tight

Cause I can't hold it anymore.
I need you to be,
The colour to my drawing
Cause I can't be empty anymore.
I need you to,
Love me again
Cause I can't feel nothing anymore.

-Mahi

Ajnabi se the tum,
Zindagi baan gaye.
Meri duniya mai aake,

Mere humsafar baan gaye.
Bewaja si thi meri zindagi,
Jeene ki wajha tum baan gaye.
Mere haar khushi ki,
Wajha tum baan gaye.
Magar waqt badal gya,
Aur tum bhi.
Ab mere totne ki wajha,
tum baan gaye.
Dard deene ki wajha,

Tum baan gaye.
Mere humsafar se...
Wapas, ajnabi tum baan guess.
-Mahi

Shruti

My name is Shruti Dayal, I was born on 14 December 1999, in the city of nawabs 'Lucknow', I am a neet aspirant I want to become a doctor who can heal and help the needy people, My hobbies are painting, reading novels, writing songs and writing  about stuff about the society or emotions in the form of poems, I have started writing poems at the age of 11, from that moment till today my passion of writing has never stopped.

Self Love

The only person that you have to the treat the best is You,

because you are the only one who stay with you from your birth till the day of your death,

No one can understand you, protect you, care about you, be a well wisher for you and be a soulmate of you, better than YOU.

So, always love yourself, because you have to travel miles and go far away from where you are with yourself....

-Shruti

Conversion between Me &???

Don't be unhappy,
you are lucky to have me,
I will not come and go,
like seashore flow,
in hard times you haven't known.
I will be happy if you are happy,
I will be sad when you are sad.
I will hard when you work harder,
Never leave you in rough weather.
You are stronger than me,

You are wiser than me,
You are always more than you believe.
Don't do any wrong intentionally,
or you can't see into my eyes bravely.
Love yourself and embrace your beauty,
only then I can love you without feeling guilty.
You are strong, You are brave,you can have whatever you
want if you work for it.
Yes you can do it,
Yes you can do it.
After this, I kissed it happily as i am a biggest supporter
of me,

Yes i kissed the mirror hanging on the wall with perfection,
cause it was all said by my reflection.
-Shruti

Sapphire

Its just a bad day,
its doesn't mean you are bad in any way.
People will laugh at you,
cause they are unaware of your view.
They doubt your potential,
but you know their words are not essential.

Focus on yourself,
achieve everything that you want at your shelf.
Never think yourself lesser than anyone,
cause your dreams are known by none.
Work harder than you can ever think,
because not everyone has high links.
Have faith on your hard work,
as it always beats golden luck.
Don't be angry on Hater's crew,
let your success speaks on behalf of you.
At last convert your spark,

into a forest fire,

and burn yourself until you became a Sapphire.

-Shruti

The Time When I Was Me

The when I was me,

 was the time when I was really me.

I don't have to worry about things that wasn't free,

I used to roam like a honey bee.

The time when I was me,

was the time when I can be me.

there was no kind of formality,
to be good with those who can't understand my mentality.
The time when I was me,
was the time when I can feel the beauty of me.
there was no layer of makeup,
or fear of breakup.
The time when I was me,
was the time when I was the happiest version of me.
there was no worries of society's cult,

or being called as a slut.
The time when I was me,
was the time when I want to be in,
but now the real me have been buried in a burning field,
and I and been reincarnated as someone that's wasn't
me,
real laughter replaced by fake smiles,
bitter truth replaced by sweet lies,
reckless runs replaced by cautious steps,
The time when I was me,
was the time I was really me.

-Shruti

Remembering the Old Days

Remembering the old days is not a part of mine,
but still I remember the old art of the time.

I used to crawl when I am 8 months old and all my own,
to explore the world which I haven't known.

I used to ask what is this,
what is that,
but still not aware why is this,
why is that.

I grew and what attracts me was

cartoons, Mr Bean and Mr Frank,
was number 1 in the rank.
Doremon and Perman was adorable man,
Shin Chan and Hugemarru was mischievous brats and
Mogli and Chacha Chaudhry done a marvelous jobs in
our breath.

Few years later cartoon has lost its craze,
what is active in the race is fantacy, horror and
adventurous novels,
Ruskin Bond, Ronald Dahl is all time favorite,
and Nancy Drew,Goosebumps is 100% in the rate.

Parents acts as a support,

for everyone in there life,
whenever I fell they encourages me to stand up all alone
and making me brave,
as they will not stay with me till my grave.

After that what is ahead is not memorable for me,
 as I turn 65 from 3.

Now I am lying in my bed and rather counting my left
days I am remembering the Old Days
-Shruti

Yu-Ming (Jackson) Chang

Jackson Chang is an MA student enrolled in the English Program at the National Central University in Taiwan. He is interested in children's literature, poetry and translation. Jackson has been writing poetry since 2018 and admires the work of Rabindranath Tagore, famous for his poems and songs, and for being the first Asian to win the Noble Prize in 1913.

A Genius's Loneliness

He was known to be the wisest in the history of existence
He was just bound to be right, no matter the resistance
He got a gift to live in a mysterious dream
Or maybe he was just trapped, where no one could hear his silent screams.
They called him insane but he was a free soul
He loved his life like a crazy lover, no matter what he was told
His innocence felt so real and true

He had faith in himself that he would make it through.
He was like a miraculous happening only once to be found
He was strange and was born to turn the world around
Curiosity made him wander off to strange places in his mind
He went on looking for strange stuff that he was always meant to find.
-Jackson

A Generous King

His divine soul was like a star in the sky
His heart was drenched in truth in that ocean of the lies
He was strong cuz he was forged in pain
Today he ruled cuz he never stopped when it rained.
To sit quiet and be nice wasn't kinda his thing
He was known to all as the mighty sarcasm king
He had a friendly embrace and a smile on his face

He played Mr. nice in each and every case.

He was just so kind and cared for every soul

His heart was a heavenly spark which shone its light on all

Curiosity made him wander off to strange places in his mind

He went on looking for strange stuff that he was always meant to find.

He was like a miraculous happening only once to be found

He was strange and was born to turn the world around

He had the heart of a lion and the vision of a king
He had no fear left now, so weakness wasn't his thing.
He was so wild but he had a beating heart
His savage way to live was like an only art
He forged himself to be clever cuz the weak didn't survive
He was the mastermind behind the hunt cuz he was meant to thrive.
-Jackson

A kind Swan

Kindness sort of dwell in her heart
She had a dream to turn the world into art
It was more than just a pretty face she had
She was the sun in the evening going red.
She had a smile, only one of a kind
It was just so beautiful, like a happy illusion of the mind
Honesty wasn't just her habit, it was the way of her life
The truth on her tongue sometimes felt sharper than the knife.

She had that charm and the beauty of the queen
She was the bright streak of light that only night had seen
Her love for written words was one of a kind
She had lived all those fantasies ever set up in a clever mind.
She had a kind and caring heart
She was a gift of nature's living art
She was so divine and goodness brimmed her heart
She went on helping others like ray of light in the dark.

She didn't let go of her humanity even though her heart
bleed
And hid the pain in the pages of a book that no one was
supposed to read
She had a friendly smile and a warm embrace
With that young and stupid heart, she aspired a heavenly
grace.
She possessed a dragon's heart
That courage she had was a heavenly moonspark
Her wings were on fire, she was always meant to rise
She was a queen born to avenge the skies.

-Jackson

Enthusiastic Deer

She had a friendly smile and a warm embrace
With that young and stupid heart, she aspired a heavenly grace
She was a fun loving and life living girl
Her funny nature was as precious as a piano black pearl.
She possessed a dragon's heart
That courage she had was a heavenly moonspark
She didn't let go of her humanity even though her heart bleed

And hid the pain in the pages of a book that no one was supposed to read.
The best thing about her was the goodness in her soul
She was the shadow of a divine goddess standing tall
Her wings were on fire, she was always meant to rise
She was a queen born to avenge the skies.
She was so divine and goodness brimmed her heart
She went on helping others like ray of light in the dark

Her curiosity led her to the places she's never been before
It was the beat in her heart and the reason she was breathing for.
Kindness sort of dwell in her heart
She had a dream to turn the world into art
It was more than just a pretty face she had
She was the sun in the evening going red.
Honesty wasn't just her habit; it was the way of her life
The truth on her tongue sometimes felt sharper than the knife

She had that charm and the beauty of the queen
She was the bright streak of light that only night had seen.

-Jackson

Immortal Warrior (Gladiator)

He was strong cuz he was forged in pain
Today he ruled cuz he never stopped when it rained
His silence spoke louder than words
Like clinging swords in the battle of the worlds.

He was heroic and so very fearless
He was the perfect man with that touch so deep
He wished to free from the Colosseum with paying any cost
He loved to explore new horizons to life, without a thought of hesitation.
He had a friendly embrace and a smile on his face
He battled with Achilles in each and every case
He was just so kind and cared for every soul
His heart was a heavenly spark which shone

its light on the Greek Underworld.

He had the heart of a lion and the vision of a king

He had no fear left now, so weakness wasn't his thing

He was like a miraculous happening only once to be found in the Colosseum

He was glorious and was born to turn the world around.

-Jackson

Kamalika Sanyal

This is Kamalika Sanyal originally hailing from Kolkata but she has been residing in Bangalore for the past 6 years and currently working as a procurement analyst for Google. Writing for her has always been a potent medium of self expression and sense of being heard when jotting down words..

Rhythm:

The tune of serendipity floated through the conundrum of reality.

He who played the chords lurked but only in obscurity

His fingers glided through the subliminal as the tuned rippled, the music of the heart that got the odds crippled.

A musician in his own rights has the allegiance of possibilities.

A man who stood tall in his endless abilities.

The artist besotted with the passion of nature, he would have sold a sunset for a thousand of musical sunrises.

The rhythm divine had the causes to nurture.

A walk in the washed sand; collecting shells of sizes with guitar strung across and lips

parted in hums, a musician with the tune of serenity marches to his own drums.

-For music knows no reason but only the celebration-

-Kamalika Sanyal

An Ode To A Dream:

I traverse like a silhouette through the canopy of myriad of bewilderment.
Introspective of my actions, I weave cascading thoughts.
Through the nooks and crannies of sublime conscience, I walk the eternity.
At times I am inane; unwinding a child's mind and at times I breath into a genius's incandescent perceptions.
More potent than fact, I have been long working up magic throughout.
My fidelity to the dream-catcher, the

enchanter and that little boy who embarks on changing the world, to the entangled wishes and the distraught hearts.

To the finesse of love; I am a dream, a trance!

A dreamer holds the mythological cords of the realms!-

-Kamalika Sanyal

Bonita:

She works up myriad of ripples in the heart.

The bold reflection swipes up the wind.

Her graceful gait that flatters you .

The face that bears the lines of wise conscience, the eyes that loves many but belongs to the one, the lips that kiss like a thunderstorm.

To the potent and the amicable soul that leaves you feeling loved and her gratuitous nature that gives into you.

She is all you have long desired, the make-believe love making.

Her voice echoes through the subtle breath of life.

Her words that can ameliorate the most unconcerned of the minds.

The smile she wears as an armor through her

journey, She is You, she is a Woman!

The line of consistency, the fathom of your naive judgments and the chord of your existence.

Reflections should be bold....Attitude should be encouraging and Grace should be commanding.-

-Kamalika Sanyal

Prologue:

To the Life and its sanctity.

To the first breath of genesis.

Delineating the harmony of humanity.

The revelation of time and tide of survival, for I am the prologue, the inexorable, I am Death!

When Life's conscience approves the conduct of the living; I am then but a dissuasion, a threshold into the beyond.

For I have passed over through centuries, have seen empires rise and effigies fall.

To the Gods and the all of mankind, I have

always hold an affinity, to the reality and the delusion I am the only truth; a winged demon biding my time.

To the moment when I waltz my way with my fair lady through, holding her close to the bosom, drawing her breath.

In that one last look of longing, of hope, I have pulverized life for she is now dead; and I have again conjured up yet another spirit.

For its me you are incarnated and to me you shall return!

-Kamalika Sanyal

Supraja v p

supraja she is from chennai tamilnadu . she works in a reputed mnc in chennai. she was more into stories since childhood, so she started writing  since then but couldn't continue. Her hobbies include reading,singing,watchingmovies.

Quotes

Flower

People think I'm always delicate by seeing my petals but they forget that i hold thorns too.

Life is not to thrive & survive but live

Enjoy the rain now , later rainbow may be the outcome when the sun shines.

Life is all about acceptance than expectancy.

-Supraja v p

Comparison is the theft of joy.

I wish school's taught these simple things when you are at your youngest. Each lives matter and each lives are different from one and another. Some might have known the phrase " im best in my own way". I think teachers must motivate children to be the best version of themeselves . So that each child would have their own spark."Comparison is the mother of failure". It doesn't let you grow and sometimes it kills the soul that am i not enough ? The way i am to attitre a dream it holds in its mind. Or the crave of its self being to be on its own way. The sad part is it does not let self love flourish in the mind it blocks it. Remain on mute as youre an average none of your words will be heared or valued. People like good looks more than good thoughts. Were does the complex phase, arise in this world to let one down and feel lower self -esteem. ,people's words play a huge part . "You judge someone's story you haven't been a part of you know just like the way picking a book going through the chapter's half phase of the book you left behind were the story still remains "unknown". Everyone has flaws people just hide it better in different inter phase (stages). Or in different ways. Everyone wants to be perfect and everyone wants to be liked while they forget that , Even god does not acquire that power to be liked by all.Im nor saying you're wrong our opinions are as they differ from one and another. I have a different prespective of thinking and knowledge of the world I've seen and people i have known so have you too. Everything we follow is an example, if we teach some basic things along with education might change we are the people and we are the one's who represent the society belong so let us be the change and bring the change.So that no other child would feel inferior about themselvef each one would support each other for their own welfare. Education will not only present in the books and minds alone by circular agenda. Also through behaviour too.

-Supraja v p

Anushka chouhan

Anushka is a teen writer from Madhya Pradesh, she has delusion fascination of glass and literature, perhaps aspiring civil services. Education- DPS'19 DAVV'22

The Millennial Connection

Hey! I'm Kia, as the name suggests a riser, assertive and bossy. Way back then I was devastated and shook in life, my soul used to shudder every now and then. You might be wondering why?

I was dating a toxic individual and this write up is highly recommended to the people who are encountering similar life experiences.

'I dance, I scream, I spin and fall
Though all inside the cerebral hall,
My eyes had a tinge of red mice,
Oh! My heart cries more than my eyes.'

Its hard when you keep things to yourself initially but, it later makes you invulnerable. You have the solution of your every problem, it's only you who would wipe your tears at the end of the day.

'Maybe the arms I fought for were never mine,
I was running out of peace and he was still blooming on his conceit.'

There is always this one person for whom we extend our limits, give unconditional love, have eminence faith but what for?
What if that one person was never ours?
If they ain't reverting emotions to you, back off!

'Dreamt of a soul connection with you,
You somehow chose the canvas.'

Expecting a pure bond in this world of

hookups is no less a foolish act. It's not that all I wanted was him but I craved for his efforts too. Real is rare.

'It was a myth I was consoling my heart to believe.
Now I'm silent, I'm prude from euphoric years to crestfallen roots,
The comparison between the two you made has left nothing but a dark shade.'

We all sometimes force our hearts to believe in things that ain't true, we live in a delusional world that is satisfied by lovely thoughts, way far from reality.
This is the main reason of annihilation of

ones elation and initiation of depression.

If they compare you with other people frequently or measure your degree
of affection, back off!

'May be the heart that cried has no tears left,
May be the soul that suffered has no hopes left.'
'Thanks for making me realise that being in love and
being happy are two different things.'

There is a time when you reach the climax. Fear no loss,
it's the end not of your lively

happiness but of your misery. You deserve all the happiness of the world, of your life and if someone tries to snatch that away, back off!

'Heal! Until your happiness stop depending on them.'

The stuff that can make you happy is your own thought of being happy.
It's your aura, your vibe, your family, your friends don't just depend on a
single source of happiness.

'I'm still
Since the time I left you
Memories kept pulling me down in filth

I'm not moving anymore
But in head.
I'm still
Since I hung up
Thought of loosing you kept haunting me
But now I realise
I never had you.

I'm still
Now what to fear
What to loose
I'm breathing again

Way far from booze.

Now you can never leave
My heart blue.'
 Heart breaks are significant, it pulls out the best version of you, it gives you
 courage, it makes you fearless and affirm on your goals.
 That's when you begin empathising the value of loving yourself.
 Perhaps the best phase of life!

A gratitude to self-love,

When was the last time you considered yourself superior
in life apart from your Instagram feed ?
Or may I ask about your shattered wills aiming to fly high
somehow beyond the gloomy days?
Last I heard him was two years ago begging for love, to
be loved in faith of ransacking soul.
In urge of praise I was ready to be an option (last mistake
).
Timid chicks not liking their face,
From skinny edges to lethal fat we all someway struggled

.

Wish I was one shade fairer, damn I have a short stature-stuff people often crib about.

All you'll ever need lies within you, the moment you have to cherish is now, once you shine brighter your confidence boost, you act with love, you acknowledge your own company, you fall in love with yourself that's how you grow. Just believe in you!

'I'm living

Behind the shadow of life

Spots on me

CO-stars scrounging my vision

Though clasping back

A beam penetrated my heart

That was you
Messed and sad
Thoughts swirled my head
Let's cure this light
Sight hindered
Pieces cracked
Often ended in gloom
I'll come back
Strengthen and powerful
I'm invincible
Will destroy you.'

Some incidences give you a life long lesson, some hypocrites will just try to pull you down. We often try to heal others and during that process we end up hurting ourself. Not all you hear is true and not all you suspect is false.

You'll fall but recovery is a surety and you'll come back more powerful than ever before now, you are invincible.Now that I've expertise in this field I'll define love for you.

Yes, love exist!

It's the highest form of affection you have for someone. The bells in heart, the tunes of violin or the butterflies are nothing but a CLICK considered hike in oxytocin, dopamine and serotonin level in the body.

(First realisation).

You often loose and gain things in love.

You care, you own, you stretch your limits, you give, you happen to do stuff you never thought of doing, you bond, you glow, you feel elated like never before is the first phase.

You shatter, you devastate, you beg, you choke, you feel helpless, your heart ache, you are hurt, you die of jealousy, your soul

stink like a rotten egg is the other.

You can't love the same person twice but can love more than twice.

The next click would ensue indeed maybe after a year or four.

Like the energy is never created nor destroyed your affection shifts from one to other meantime you heal.

That's life!

A person just occupies a space in your heart that hurts if happen to be void.

Fill up the blacks!

Don't ever fall for words, your value as person is significant and the things that are

meant to be yours would find it's way and will STAY.

If you are not getting enough attention from them, leave.

If you are mere a secret they are hiding from their circle, leave.

If your tears doesn't affect their deeds, leave.

If you are not their priority, leave.

If they are not initiating efforts to make to stay, leave.

If their words and actions are contradictory, leave.

If they make you think a little less of you, leave.

If they are just exploiting you for mental or physical satisfaction, leave.

If you are dating a toxic individual, Just LEAVE.

 'Whole is you, way I can give.'
~ I'm just a mediator between you and your happiness. I can brief you with the means to escape, execution is your part.
'Don't take shit' if I talk in your words.

Cleanse your aura.

That was my story, where are you?
Think Mellow! Thrive Mellow!
-Anushka Chouhan

Tanghiu Longshe

Tanghiu Longshe is from Pathso village. He belongs to Khiamniungan Naga community from Nagaland. He developed his love for writing at the age of 18. It was his interest in music that first inspired him to began his writing in the form of lyrics. Later he was further inspired to keep writing by the pain and suffering that is face by the humanity to express his thoughts and emotions to the people around him.

His writings are more about understanding life. He writes as a seeker rather than just a believer.

Servants of Nature

Birth give us an opportunity to live and be merry
But it also gives us a chance to walk through hell.
Whenever we face pain and suffering
We shall not blame birth,
She is just the servant of nature.

Death give us an opportunity to rest
But it also gives us a chance to see our loved ones dies,
But we shall not blame death,
She is just the servant of nature.

It is the nature that controls the world,
She gives and she takes back,
We shall be willing to let go and give what belongs to her.
We shall not complain,
It only brings pain and suffering,
We are just the servants of nature.

- Tanghiu Longshe

The Best Night

On a cold winter morning
I set out for a journey.
As I stepped out of my door
The warm sun shone down on me.
I looked up to the sky in joy
And she gently whispered to my ear,
" You can have my warmness everyday as long as you live.
Keep living".
As I walked along the barren road
The trees stood tall along the side of the road shading me
form the burning mid-day sun.

I set down for a rest under them
And heard them whispered,
"You can enjoy our shade as long as you live.
Keep living".
As the night slowly took over the twilight
I completed my journey.
I laid down on my bed in peace thanking the sun and the
trees for the day
And the dark night gently whispered to my ear saying,
"The sun is coming back to keep you warm. The trees are
busy growing to give you shade.
Just rest in peace into my arms until dawn."

As I laid still silently into the night
The future came whispering to my ear saying,
"The best days of your life lays in me.
Every experience you made everyday is adding wisdom to
your life.
Just keep up the pace
You don't know how wise you have become in me".
I laid still silently into the night
And the old age came to me and said,
"You have the privilege to meet your children and your
grandchildren in me.
The respect that comes along with gray hair is yours if you
come living into me".

I laid still silently into the night
Watching enthusiasm that was taking root in me,
The excitement that was getting louder for living,
It was one of the best nights of my life
But the best days of my life lays in the future.
- Tanghiu Longshe

City on a hill

Dear me,
We traveled so far from where we used to be,
We wandered through the hills and valleys
Until we saw a city set on a hill
Giving light to the world.
Now we are drawing our old-self
Into cold water,
We are learning to crawl and walk,
We are standing to follow His lead,
Nothing could satisfy us
But be the city on a hill.
We will never stop
Until He say well done,
We will never stop
Until He calls us back home,
We shall forever be His light.
We were made to be the city on a hill.
We traveled so far from where we used to be,
We finally found a fountain that never runs dry.
We no longer ask why
But in everything with faith we rest.
We were made to be the city on a hill.
-Tanghiu Longshe

Dear Sunshine

Dear Sunshine,
I'm pouring out my heart
taking to my diary about you.
Every night we talk about you,
Tonight she finally know that you heart me all.

All my life I've been looking for
I finally found in you.

When you're around
My sky is alway bright even when it rains.
When you're around

You make me feel like no one else could do.
When you're around
Words can't express, all I can say is my life is complete.

Every day the sun rise high
But it will never shine without you.
You are my sunshine.
- Tanghiu Longshe

I RATHER BE

I'm a busy man
Not in a way they think I'm,
There is a world within me

Where my body do not exist.
I'm a busy seeker
Discovering myself in there.

They think I'm just the body and a mind
But little do they know
I just own this body for sometime
But it's not me.
My mind is just the product
Produce by my brain.

They number the age of my life
Beginning from the day I was born,
But can they be sure

Life never happens first
In the hands of the creator even before in the womb?

They say nobody gets out alive,
No wise nor fool from this world.
But death is for my body and my mind.
After all,
I'm beginning to feel like a fool to them
But I rather be
Because nothing compares to the place where my soul dwells.

- Tanghiu Longshe

COMPILER KUMKUM PRIYADARSHINI SAHU

She is a chemist doing her graduation in kalahandi University. She has the great passion for literature. She can pen down her emotions in various manner with proper wordings. She is fully dedicated towards her dream and passion. She has a great sense of humour towards understanding right emotions of people. She has a great interest towards literature. She loves to relish her emotions through ink.

Bshayar52 is a community which provides his/her writers, an unimaginable platform. Every writer has a dream to publish his/her works one day and keep his book of thoughts open, in front of the world. Bshayar52 is that one community that aims to fulfil such unimaginable dreams of such writers. It aims to provide the writers, the best opportunity possible! "EACH PERSON HAS HIS OWN STORY, SORROW OR GLORY" similarly each writer has 'something' to say to the world; something it needs to change with his pen! This community provides the golden chance to raise their voices, without any fear of being told to shut up! I am proud to be a part of such a community which is growing day by day, dreaming to fulfil others' dreams... Bshayar52 is not only a community; it's a family with great responsibility. It's connected with deep emotion; we are dedicated towards it with strong devotion. It's the finest milestones which lead us towards success. It encourages us to explore our feelings without any stress or worries about being judged by people. Writers with us and make your image globally. We as a team are very greedy, greedy for talent, talented writers. For us our team is everything and we as a team try to search every nook and corner for that one writer who would swell us with pride. We are not afraid of the penance. We await the beautiful pieces. We accept every writer amateur or professional; we are here for the writing community.

We also provide knowledge and training to present your emotions and how to publish it. We are here to increase your worthiness by organizing daily weekly and monthly challenges. Be a published writer, only with Bshayar52! We